Grandy Thaxter's Helper

Written by Douglas Rees

Grandy Thaxter's Helper

Illustrated by S. D. Schindler

Atheneum Books for Young Readers
New York   London   Toronto   Sydney

Atheneum Books for Young Readers

An imprint of Simon & Schuster Children's Publishing Division

1230 Avenue of the Americas

New York, New York 10020

Book design by Kristin Smith and Daniel Roode

The text of this book is set in Cheltenham.

The illustrations are rendered in gouache, watercolor, and ink.

Manufactured in China

First Edition

10 9 8 7 6 5 4 3 2 1

Library of Congress Cataloging-in-Publication Data

Rees, Douglas.

Grandy Thaxter's helper / by Douglas Rees ; illustrated by S. D. Schindler.—1st ed.

p.   cm.

Summary: When Death shows up to take her away, Grandy Thaxter finds so much work for him to do that he decides to come back when she is not so busy.

ISBN 0-689-83020-3

[1. Grandmothers—Fiction. 2. Death—Fiction. 3. Work—Fiction.]

I. Schindler, S.D., ill. II. Title.

PZ7.R25475 Gr 2003

[E]—dc21   2001045818

For Marian
—D. R.

To Charlotte
—S. D. S.

Grandy Thaxter took care of children. She took care of her own grandchildren, Patience, Prudence, and Perseverance. She also took care of the other children in town who didn't have anyone else to take care of them. Their names were Joel, Joshua, Jacob, and Jeroboam. The work was hard and long, but Grandy Thaxter didn't know any other kind, and the children loved her. Everyone was happy.

One day, when Grandy Thaxter was alone, a man came to the house. He was tall and pale and dressed in fine black clothes. "Hello, Grandy," he said. "I'm Mister Death. I've come to carry you away with me."

Not likely, thought Grandy.

"I can't go until I finish my work," she said. "If you give me a hand, I can leave sooner."

"All right," said Mister Death. "What do I have to do?"

"This is an easy day," said Grandy. "Just give me a little help around the house."

She gave Mister Death a broom and he went to work. He swept all the floors and all the corners. When he was done, the boards shone like new. But Mister Death was sneezing from the dust.

"Can we go now?" asked Mister Death.

"Nice job," said Grandy. "But you forgot to do the ceilings and the closets."

So Mister Death went back and swept down the cobwebs and cleaned
the closets. Meanwhile, Grandy polished the furniture. When Mister Death was
finished, his nose was running and his eyes were full of tears from the dust. He
said, "Are you ready to go now, Grandy?"

"The windows," said Grandy.

So Mister Death took ashes and water and mixed them together the way Grandy told him to do. Then he washed all the windows in the big old house. When he was done, they gleamed like jewels. But his hands were sore and puckered. He was tired. Mister Death thought about how far he had to carry Grandy.

"You know," he said, "I could come back tomorrow."

"I'll be ready for you," Grandy said.

The next day Mister Death came back bright and early. "Are you ready to go with me now, Grandy?" he asked.

"You know," said Grandy, "if I'm going to go with you, I'd better get the laundry done first."

Grandy pulled out all the dirty clothes and put them in the yard. They made a pile higher than the roof.

"This will take all day," Mister Death said.

"It will go faster if you help," Grandy said.

Mister Death looked at the mountain of dirty laundry. "What do we have to do?" he asked.

"First, we make soap," Grandy said.

Grandy brought out a big black kettle. She sent Mister Death into the forest to gather wood to pile under it. Then she made a layer of ashes at the bottom of the kettle. She laid bundles of straw on top of this and poured thick grease over the straw. "Now you try," she said.

Mister Death made more layers of ashes, straw, and grease. They got all over his fine black clothes. The straw made him itch.

When the kettle was as full as Grandy wanted it, she gave Mister Death two buckets and sent him to the well for water. The buckets were heavy, the water was heavy, and Mister Death had to make a lot of trips to fill the kettle. By the time he was done, his shoulders hurt.

Grandy lit the fire and handed Mister Death a big wooden paddle. A horrible smell rose from the kettle.

"Ugh," said Mister Death.

"Stir," said Grandy.

Mister Death and Grandy stirred until everything was boiled together. When they were done, Mister Death's fine clothes smelled like the soap. His arms were tired from using the paddle. His eyes were red from the smoke. His nose was running again.

"Now what?" Mister Death asked.

"While the soap is cooling, we start dinner," Grandy said.

Grandy got a big pile of corn and a grinder. "Just put the corn in and turn the crank," she said.

Mister Death ground all the corn.

By the time he was finished, his shoulders hurt even more. His right arm was more tired than his left and he had a blister on his hand.

"I could pop that with a pin," Grandy said.

"No, thanks," Mister Death said.

Grandy put a big black kettle on the fireplace. She sent Mister Death back to the well for more water. By the time the kettle was full, his blister was bigger, his shoulders hurt even more, and his legs were tired.

Grandy put the cornmeal and some salt into the kettle. She lit the fire under it and handed Mister Death a ladle. "Just keep stirring," she said.

After a long time, the corn boiled into mush.

"Good work," said Grandy. "Now let's finish those clothes."

"What do we have to do?" asked Mister Death.

"Washing clothes is easy," Grandy said.

First they had to clean out the soap kettle. Next they filled it with water again, put the soap and the clothes in, and stirred them around until they were clean. Then they rinsed the clothes in clean water, and spread them on bushes to dry.

There were many loads to wash. Mister Death worked hard and tried to do a good job, but he burned his hand on the kettle. Grandy had to make him a poultice for it.

By the time they were done, Mister Death's fine clothes were wet from the washing. His hands were more puckered than ever from the hot, soapy water. He was very, very tired.

"Are you ready now, Grandy?" Mister Death asked.

"Here come the children home from school," Grandy said.

Prudence, Patience, and Perseverance, Joel, Jacob, Joshua, and Jeroboam came running into the yard.

"Kids, this is Mister Death," Grandy said. "Be respectful to him and keep out of his way. He's helping me today."

"Hi," said the children. "When do we eat?"

It was a little bit early for supper, but they had it anyway. Mister Death sat down with them and had cornmeal mush.

"Good mush," said Patience.

"Very good mush," said Prudence.

"Exceptionally good mush," said Perseverance.

"Extremely good mush," said Joel.

"Wonderful mush," said Jacob.

"Best mush I ever tasted," said Joshua.

"Best mush in the world," said Jeroboam.

Mister Death blushed with pleasure. "Thank you," he said. "I made it."

"Thank *you*," they all said.

After supper Grandy sent the children out to bring in the laundry. "I'll do the dishes tonight," she said to them.

Mister Death sighed. "Can I help?"

"Of course," Grandy said.

So Mister Death took the buckets again and went down to the well. He had to bring back many buckets of water. He filled the big black kettles that had made the soap and the cornmeal mush. Grandy heated the water and scoured out one of the kettles. Mister Death scoured the other.

By the time they were finished, Mister Death's hands were red and raw from the scouring.

"It's getting dark," Mister Death said. "Are you going to be ready soon?"

"Just as soon as we finish the dishes," Grandy said.

So Mister Death went back to the well for more water. He filled the kettles and Grandy heated the water again. They washed the dishes in one kettle and rinsed them in the other.

"You are a lot of help," said Grandy. "I wish you could stay."

"Um," said Mister Death.

At last the dishes were done. Grandy put the children to bed.

Mister Death sat down in a big soft chair. "I am tired," he said. "I need to rest a little while before I carry you away."

"Good idea," said Grandy.

Mister Death woke up later when the room grew cold. Grandy was sitting across from him, smiling.

"Did you have a good nap?" she asked.

Mister Death shook his head. He still felt tired. His arms and legs were still sore. His shoulders and blister and burn still hurt. He thought about how far he had to carry Grandy.

He got up and went to the door. "Tomorrow," he said softly. "First thing tomorrow."

When Mister Death came back the next morning, the yard was full of big, heavy tools. There were huge piles of wet reeds tied into bundles. Grandy Thaxter was there. So were Prudence, Patience, and Perseverance, Joel, Joshua, Jacob, and Jeroboam.

"What's all this?" Mister Death asked.

"We're making flax for linen," the children said.

"We're going to brake it and swingle the reeds to get the flax," said Joel, Joshua, Jacob, and Jeroboam.

"We're going to hackle it and spin it," said Prudence, Patience, and Perseverance.

"So I can weave it into cloth," said Grandy.

"But that could take all day," Mister Death said.

"It will go faster if you help," Grandy said.

"We'll let you use the big swingler," the boys said. "It will be fun."

"But come and have breakfast first," Grandy said.

Mister Death looked at the big, heavy tools. He looked at the huge piles of wet reeds.

He thought about how tired he was and how much he still hurt. He thought about his burn and his blister.

"No, Grandy," said Mister Death. "I will come back some time when you are not so busy."

"That will be fine," said Grandy.

All the children laughed. They knew Grandy Thaxter was always busy.

And she still is, right to this very day.